Fairy Bears
Primrose

'I promise to do my best. I promise to
work hard to care for the world and
all its plants, animals and children.
This is the Fairy Bear Promise."

Look out for more magical Fairy Bears!

Dizzy

Sunny

Blossom

Sparkle

Primrose

Misty

Lulu

Poppy

Visit the secret world of the Fairy Bears and explore the magical Crystal Caves . . .

www.fairybearsworld.com

Fairy Bears

Primrose

Julie Sykes

Illustrated by Samantha Chaffey

MACMILLAN CHILDREN'S BOOKS

First published 2010 by Macmillan Children's Books
a division of Macmillan Publishers Limited
20 New Wharf Road, London N1 9RR
Basingstoke and Oxford
Associated companies throughout the world
www.panmacmillan.com

ISBN 978-0-330-51205-3

1 3 5 7 9 8 6 4 2

A CIP catalogue record for this book is available from
the British Library.

Printed and bound in the UK by CPI Mackays, Chatham ME5 8TD

For Sarah, my big little sis

Prologue

At the bottom of Firefly Meadow, not far from the stream, stands a tall sycamore tree. The tree is old with a thick grey trunk and spreading branches. Hidden amongst the branches is a forgotten squirrel hole. If you could fly through the squirrel hole and down the inside of the tree's hollow trunk, you would find a secret door that leads to a special place. Open the door and step inside the magical Crystal Caves, home of the Fairy Bears.

The Fairy Bears are always busy. They work hard caring for nature and children everywhere. You'll have to be quick to see them, and you'll have to believe in magic.

Fairy Bears

Do you believe in Fairy Bear magic? Can you keep a secret? Then come on in – the Fairy Bears would love to meet you.

Chapter One

The class cave was empty when Primrose the Fairy Bear slipped inside. Primrose was always the first to arrive and she stood for a moment, her green wings quivering excitedly as she breathed in the familiar smell of the stone seats, tables and leaf note books. Primrose loved school! There was nothing better than putting her brain to work on the problems and puzzles that Miss Alaska set each day. Hurrying over to the teacher's desk she sorted through the pile of maths books until she found her own.

"Ten out of ten and a honey bee point!"
sighed Primrose happily. Honey bee points
were given as a reward for good work or
good behaviour. Later
Miss Alaska would give
Primrose a bee-shaped
token to put in her honey
jar, and once the jar
was full Primrose could
exchange the tokens for
a jar of real honey.

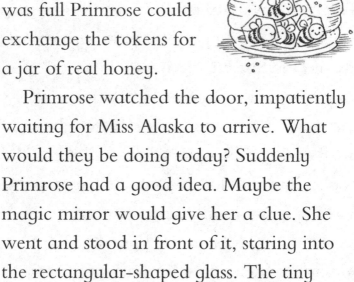

Primrose watched the door, impatiently
waiting for Miss Alaska to arrive. What
would they be doing today? Suddenly
Primrose had a good idea. Maybe the
magic mirror would give her a clue. She
went and stood in front of it, staring into
the rectangular-shaped glass. The tiny
crystals decorating the frame sparkled
brightly.

A Puzzle for Primrose

"What are you trying to tell me?"
Primrose wondered aloud. But all she could
see was her own reflection: a happy bear
with striking gold fur and bright green
wings. Suddenly her reflection flickered and
then changed to show a cute white dog
curled up on a tartan rug. His nose rested
on his paws and there was a sad expression
on his whiskery face.

"Oh!" cried Primrose. "You poor thing.
Whatever can be wrong?"

The dog gave a deep sigh, but the mirror
was changing again. In a swirl of green
the little dog disappeared and the mirror
switched to a picture of a young girl sitting
in her bedroom colouring in a picture of
a basket of puppies. Primrose thought the
girl looked friendly. She had black hair
neatly plaited, which fell over one shoulder,
and the tip of her tongue stuck out of her

mouth as she concentrated. Primrose's eyes widened at the different shades of colouring pencils the girl was using, each one engraved with her name, Lucy.

"Hello, Lucy," whispered Primrose.

A Puzzle for Primrose

She knew Lucy couldn't hear, but she watched her thoughtfully until the picture disappeared and her own reflection returned.

"What are you looking at?" asked Misty.

Primrose jumped. She'd been so engrossed by looking in the mirror that she hadn't noticed the classroom filling up.

"Hi, Misty, guess what!" she answered excitedly. "Today it's my turn to go out on a task. There's a girl called Lucy who needs my help. The mirror also showed me a picture of a sad little dog. I think the dog must belong to Lucy and she's too busy to play with him."

"Are you sure?" Misty sounded uncertain. "Miss Alaska normally gives out the tasks."

"Wait and see," said Primrose knowingly as Miss Alaska came into the classroom carrying a large sycamore leaf.

"Good morning, class." Miss Alaska smiled at the Fairy Bears. "Dizzy, stop talking and listen, please. We have a busy day ahead. Written on this leaf is a task and the name of the Fairy Bear chosen to do it."

The Fairy Bears murmured excitedly. The tasks were very important – you had to pass all of them to be allowed to move up from the junior to the senior class. Miss Alaska was working her way through the

junior class, choosing one Fairy Bear at
a time to take their first task. Primrose
wriggled excitedly on her stool, certain that
today it would be her turn!

"Before we start," said Miss Alaska,
"let's say the Fairy Bear Promise."

Stone seats grated on the cave floor as
the Fairy Bears stood up and held paws.
Standing straight, with her green wings
neatly folded behind her back, Primrose
took hold of Misty's and Lulu's paws, closed
her eyes and chanted along with the class.

"I promise to do my best. I promise to
work hard to care for the world and all its
plants, animals and children. This is the
Fairy Bear Promise."

Primrose opened her eyes as Miss Alaska
held up the sycamore leaf.

"This next task is for Primrose," she said,
smiling straight at her.

9

"Thank you," replied Primrose as she took the leaf and read it quickly.

"Just what I thought," she said confidently. "My task is to help a West Highland Terrier called Sammy who's very sad and needs cheering up."

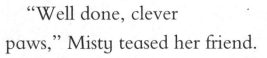

"Well done, clever paws," Misty teased her friend.

"That's not very exciting!" exclaimed Coral spitefully, wrinkling her nose. "I'm glad I didn't get that task."

"A task is as exciting as you want to make it," Primrose retorted.

She lifted her wand by its silver stem and gently rubbed the triangular-shaped jade gemstone set in its star. The green jewel sparkled brightly. Primrose waved the wand

and tiny green stars gushed out in a perfect arc.

"Well done, Primrose. That's wonderful wand work," said Miss Alaska. "Good luck, and remember to enjoy your task."

"I will," said Primrose, waving goodbye to Misty as she left the classroom.

There was a map on the sycamore leaf showing Primrose where to go once she'd left the Crystal Caves. It was a complicated journey but she was good at map reading. Primrose was also good at solving puzzles, and this one seemed easy. With a happy sigh Primrose began to rehearse what she would say to Lucy to convince her that Sammy was only sad because she was neglecting him.

Chapter Two

The Main Tunnel was full of Fairy Bears
queuing to get through the Grand Door.
Primrose landed at the back of the line
and tried not to get too frustrated at the
hold up. She was in too much of a hurry to
notice the beauty of the walls, studded with
magically sparkling jewels, or the grandness
of the gnarled root staircase at the end of
the tunnel. Primrose hopped up the staircase
and through the Grand Door, sighing
happily as she arrived inside the hollow tree
trunk that hid the Crystal Caves.

"At last!" said Primrose, her fur standing up with excitement.

Primrose blinked rapidly as her eyes adjusted to the dark. It was very quiet except for the hum of Fairy Bear wings all around her. Flapping her own wings quickly, Primrose flew upward and headed straight towards the pale circle of light shining above her. She knew it was coming from the forgotten squirrel hole, the way in and out of the sycamore tree. Primrose burst out into the daylight and sped across Firefly Meadow, not letting the lovely morning sunshine distract her.

She flew fast, enjoying the challenge of the journey. There were lots of changes in direction and each time she made a turn she hovered in the air carefully, checking the landmarks beneath her before she went on her way. A long while later Primrose

arrived at her
destination,
her furry
cheeks
flushed
with
excitement
from the
flight. The
house was a
small bungalow
with an overgrown
garden. Primrose
landed on a bush near
the gate and stared round
in surprise. This place looked far too small
and untidy to be Lucy and Sammy's home.
Hearing footsteps coming along the street
Primrose hurriedly pulled back until she was
completely hidden by leaves. The garden

gate groaned in protest as a man, dressed in a uniform and carrying a large bag, pushed it open and ran up the garden path.

"A postman," said Primrose in delight. She'd learned about them at school.

The postman was obviously in a hurry. He rammed a handful of letters into the letter box and jogged back down the garden path, leaving the gate swinging open behind him.

"Hello," called a friendly voice from the street. "Have you got any letters for us today?"

Suddenly the bush Primrose was resting on shook violently and a little white dog shot from underneath it and raced through the garden gate.

"Sammy!" exclaimed Primrose.

Gathering her wits together she flew after him.

A Puzzle for Primrose

Sammy had a limp, but he was too determined to let that stop him. He ran across the road, hurling himself at a tall girl with long black hair, standing in her front garden clutching a handful of letters.

"Hello, Sammy!" The girl bent down and patted the dog, squealing with delight as he licked her hands and face.

"You're a bad dog," she gently scolded him. "You'll get run over crossing the road like that!"

Lucy? Primrose was so surprised she forgot

to be cautious and hovered in the air. The tall girl with the serious brown eyes was definitely the same girl she'd seen in the magic mirror. So Lucy wasn't Sammy's owner. She lived on the opposite side of the road in a large house with a pretty garden and two garages! Primrose had made a mistake by jumping to conclusions and was about to make another one . . . She was completely out in the open and, catching her scent in the air, Sammy quickly spun round.

"Woof, woof, woof," he barked in a friendly greeting.

"Sammy, shh! Mum's indoors trying to work . . ." Lucy stopped mid-sentence and took a step forward. Her mouth widened into an enormous smile. "Oh! You're so pretty. At first I thought you were a bumblebee, but you look more like a fairy close up."

A Puzzle for Primrose

"I'm actually a Fairy Bear called Primrose."

Immediately Primrose knew she could trust Lucy, and she fluttered closer, hovering near the girl's pretty face.

"A Fairy Bear, that's so cute!" Lucy couldn't take her eyes off Primrose. "Are there lots of Fairy Bears?"

"Yes," said Primrose. "There are Fairy Bears all over the world."

"Even in the Arctic?" teased Lucy.

"Yes, and also Antarctica, North America, South America, Europe, Asia, Africa and Australasia." Primrose paused, trying to remember her continents.

"That's amazing," said Lucy. "So what exactly is a Fairy Bear?"

Primrose explained how Fairy Bears were related to the great bear Ursa Major and how once this great bear had helped a fairy with a damaged wing. Years later the same fairy had helped Ursa Major escape from hunters by turning him into a Fairy Bear. Lucy listened carefully.

"So Fairy Bears help animals, plants and children?" she asked when Primrose had finished explaining everything.

"That's right," said Primrose.

A Puzzle for Primrose

"Who are you helping today, or is that a secret?" asked Lucy eagerly.

Primrose hesitated. Fairy Bears were very secretive, but all her Fairy Bear friends, who'd completed their first task, had met children and made friends with them. Sparkle had even brought a girl to the Crystal Caves for a visit. But, before she could answer, the front door opened and a tall lady with long dark hair like Lucy's stepped outside.

"There you are, Lucy. What are you doing out here?"

"Hi, Mum," said Lucy, sidestepping so that she was blocking Primrose from her mother's view. "Have you finished your work?"

"I've got a bit more to do, but I'm stopping for a tea break. Would you like a drink too?"

"Yes, please. I'll have a glass of orange juice," said Lucy. "But first I've got to take Sammy back across the road to Mrs Parker. He's escaped again!"

Lucy's mum laughed. "You and your animals! Don't be too long."

Chapter Three

"Mum's an accountant," Lucy explained to Primrose as she carefully crossed the road. "She usually works in an office, but in the school holidays she's allowed to work at home. This week it's my half-term. Sometimes Mum lets me have a friend to play, but there aren't many children living around here so most of the time I'm on my own."

"That sounds lonely," said Primrose, who had lots of Fairy Bear friends living close by her home cave. In the holidays they had great fun playing in each other's caves or going out in a big group to visit the park and all the different grottos.

"It can be lonely," said Lucy. "I love animals and I'd love a dog to keep me company, but Mum and Dad won't let me have one. Mum says it wouldn't be fair to leave a dog locked up indoors when I'm at school and she's at work."

"She's right," Primrose agreed, remembering the lessons Miss Alaska had given them on animal care. "It's much better for dogs to have someone to keep them company. They get bored when they're left on their own and that's when some dogs get into mischief."

Lucy giggled.

A Puzzle for Primrose

"I know! My friend's dog Meg chews shoes when she's left alone."

"Sammy's limping," said Primrose anxiously as Lucy called the little dog to walk by her side.

"I noticed that too," said Lucy. "I haven't seen him out with Mrs Parker for days. Maybe that's why."

Primrose's brain was whirring. Her task had been to help Sammy. This must be why she was here, to cure his limp.

"Let me have a closer look," said Primrose. "Can you hold Sammy's collar and keep him still?"

"Of course," said Lucy. She crouched down and held the wriggling dog firmly by his tartan collar. "Good boy, Sammy."

Primrose fluttered down to the pavement
and examined Sammy's leg. His white fur
was so matted it was hard to see anything.
Carefully, she used the tip of her wand to
push the fur aside. The closer she got to
Sammy's paw the more he began to squirm.

"Steady, boy," said Lucy soothingly.
"Primrose is going to help you."

There was nothing wrong with the top
of the paw but it was too big and heavy for
Primrose to lift it up to look at the paw pad.
Taking a deep breath Primrose waved her
wand at Sammy's leg.

"Little Sammy, lift your paw,
Show me why it looks so sore."

As the spell ended, glittering green stars
burst from Primrose's wand and fell on
Sammy. The little dog sneezed and then his

eyes widened in surprise as his paw began
to rise in the air.

"That's amazing," Lucy gasped. "Can
you do lots of magic?"

But Primrose didn't hear. She was too
absorbed in the task of finding out what
was wrong with Sammy's leg.

"Look at that!" she exclaimed. "Poor
Sammy has a huge thorn stuck in his paw.

Lucy's plait fell over her shoulder as she bent forward to look. She pushed it away.

"Ooh! That's nasty. Sammy needs to see the vet."

"No he doesn't." Puffing out her golden chest Primrose fluttered her wings importantly. "I can sort this out."

"Is that your task?" asked Lucy.

"Yes," said Primrose, her mind racing through all the spells she knew. Removing a thorn from an animal was quite advanced magic. Primrose was flattered that Miss Alaska had chosen her for such a difficult task and determined to get it right first time. She took a slow deep breath to calm herself then, lifting her wand and pointing it at the thorn, she recited the spell.

"Nasty big thorn in Sammy's paw,
Fall out now and land on the floor."

A Puzzle for Primrose

The silver handle of Primrose's wand began to tremble. Primrose gripped it and held it tightly, even though the vibrations grew so strong they made her paw shake. There was a whooshing noise followed by a jet of green stars that rushed out of the wand's tip and fell in a glittering haze around Sammy's paw. For a few seconds Sammy's leg sparkled green. Then, as the stars evaporated, the thorn magically began to wriggle free. Eventually it fell from Sammy's paw and on to the pavement, leaving behind a nasty wound. Panting slightly Primrose rested on Lucy's hand.

"Are you OK?" asked Lucy.

"Yes, thanks, but that was strong magic. It makes you feel out of breath, like when you've been in a flying race."

Primrose pulled herself together and pointed her wand at Sammy's paw and chanted:

"As Sammy licks,
Let the wound fix."

Green stars rushed from Primrose's wand, forming a glimmering circle around Sammy's whiskery muzzle. In a daze Sammy lowered his head, stuck out his pink tongue and carefully licked his paw. With each lick the wound began to heal until there was no trace of an injury.

"Wow!" breathed Lucy. "Primrose, you are so clever."

"It was nothing," said Primrose modestly,

her brown
eyes shining
with pride.

Suddenly
Sammy
lay flat on
the ground
then,
stretching out his head, he gently nudged
Primrose with the tip of his black nose.

"That's so sweet. He's saying thank
you," declared Lucy.

"I haven't finished yet," said Primrose,
lifting her wand again.

> "*Groom Sammy until he's fluffy,*
> *Make his coat as soft as a puppy.*"

The wand shuddered then fell still. Primrose
screwed up her eyes in concentration and

chanted the words again, but still nothing happened. She almost stamped her paw with frustration.

"It's because I'm tired," she said. "I need to rest before I can do any more spells."

An excited look crossed Lucy's face.

"We don't need magic," she gabbled. "We can comb Sammy's fur with one of my doll's brushes. Wait in my front garden and I'll go and get one."

Lucy rushed indoors and a short while later came back with a small brush. Gently she combed out Sammy's knotted fur while Primrose picked out pieces of twigs and grass seeds.

"That was great fun and he looks lovely," said Lucy, standing back to admire their work. "Come on, boy. It's time to go home."

"It's time for me to go too," said

Primrose. She felt sad having to say
goodbye to Lucy so soon after meeting her,
but she was also fizzing with happiness.
She'd done it! She'd passed her first task. It
had been much easier than she'd imagined.
All her other friends had taken two days
to complete their first tasks but she'd done

hers in one. Resisting the urge to fly a somersault, in case Lucy thought she was showing off, Primrose fluttered into the air and hovered in front of Lucy.

"Do you have to go straight away?" asked Lucy. "We've only just met."

Primrose hesitated. It would be fun to play with Lucy, but what if Miss Alaska awarded her with extra marks for quickness?

"Sorry, I have to go straight home. But we can play another day."

"Really? I'd love that!" Lucy's eyes sparkled. "See you soon, Primrose."

"See you soon," said Primrose, waving her wand at Lucy as she soared into the air.

Primrose had an excellent memory. She didn't need to check the map on her sycamore leaf to find the way home. She flew fast, skilfully avoiding the winged insects flying around her, and was back at the Crystal Caves in time for lunch.

Chapter Four

Primrose hurried across the playground, her nose twitching in delight at the delicious smells coming from the dining cave. The rest of her class were already sitting at a long stone table and tucking into their meals. Primrose waved to Misty, grinning happily at the surprised look on her friend's face.

I bet she didn't expect me back so soon, thought Primrose smugly as the dinner-lady bear handed her a generous portion of honeycomb and a bowl of fruit salad. She helped herself to a glass of nectar from the drinks bar and then joined her friends.

"Squeeze up."

"It's all right, I'm not stopping. I'm going to play air ball," said Lulu, gulping down the rest of her nectar and standing up.

"Thanks, Lulu," said Primrose, sitting down next to Misty.

"Lulu is sport mad!" exclaimed Misty, her blue wings fluttering impatiently. "She didn't remember to ask you how you got on."

"Never mind," said Primrose cheerfully. "It was much easier than I thought. Sammy had a thorn in his paw so I took it out and did a healing spell, then a really nice girl called Lucy—"

"You did a healing spell!" shrieked Misty. "They're really difficult, Primrose!"

Primrose went pink with pleasure.

"I know," she said, proudly wiggling her wings.

Lunchtime passed very quickly for Primrose, who kept being asked to tell how she'd solved her first task.

"Lucy sounds really nice," said Misty wistfully. "What a shame you didn't have longer with her."

"I said I'd go and visit her again," said Primrose.

The end-of-lunch bell sounded and Primrose leaped up, eager to return to class and tell Miss Alaska her exciting news. Miss Alaska's yellow-and-pink wings fluttered in surprise when Primrose entered the class cave.

"Hello, Primrose. I didn't expect you back so soon."

Primrose blushed prettily.

"I've finished my task," she said, handing Miss Alaska the sycamore leaf that her teacher had given her earlier.

"I don't think you have," said Miss Alaska, folding her paws together and refusing to take the leaf.

Primrose wiggled the leaf at Miss Alaska.

"I have. Sammy had a thorn stuck in his

paw. I took it out and healed the wound."

"Your task was to cheer Sammy up," Miss Alaska pointed out.

"He is cheerful now the thorn's gone," insisted Primrose.

"Let me show you something," said Miss Alaska. She led Primrose to the magic mirror and made her stand in front of it.

"What do you see?"

Primrose stared at her reflection, waiting for it to disappear and show her a picture of Sammy looking happy. A swirling grey mist seeped across the mirror, clouding the glass and blotting out Primrose's image. Suddenly the mist cleared and there was Sammy curled up in his basket, with his nose on his paws, still looking very sad. Primrose was dumbstruck. Whatever was wrong with the little dog now? She stared at the picture, hoping to work it out, but

the picture was fading already and a new one forming. Here was Lucy, sprawled on a massive bean bag, totally engrossed in a book. Primrose frowned. There had to be a connection between Sammy's unhappiness and Lucy, but for the life of her Primrose couldn't see what.

An unpleasant laugh snapped Primrose out of her thoughts.

"Ha!" said Coral scornfully. "Little Miss Clever Paws is stuck for a change. How does it feel, Primrose, knowing you've failed your task?"

A Puzzle for Primrose

"Primrose hasn't failed her task. She just hasn't completed it yet," said Miss Alaska sharply. "Sometimes things aren't as obvious as they seem. You have to look deeper to find out what the true problem is."

Primrose shot Miss Alaska a grateful look. She wasn't sure what her teacher meant by looking deeper, but she was determined to try to solve the puzzle by herself.

"I'll go straight back," she said, walking to the door.

"Not today," said Miss Alaska gently. "Take the afternoon off school and go and think about what you've been asked to do."

Take the afternoon off school! Primrose opened her mouth to protest, but catching the look on Miss Alaska's face shut it again quickly. Wings drooping dejectedly she

picked up her wand
and shuffled out of
the class cave. Where
should she go? She
needed peace and
quiet to think and she
wouldn't get any at
her home cave with
her little brothers there,

who were twins and very noisy.

Not knowing where to go Primrose
wandered along the Main Tunnel, heading
in the opposite direction to the Grand Door
until she passed the play park. A tiny Fairy
Bear clutching a toy wand was playing
on the roundabout while his mum sat on
a bench reading. The swings, Primrose's
favourite park equipment, were empty.
Without thinking Primrose unlatched the
jewel-studded gate shaped like a castle door

and went into the park, sitting down on a swing. The swaying movement was very soothing. Primrose rocked back and forth idly watching the little bear playing. Faster and faster he spun the roundabout and then he leaped on, squealing with delight as he whizzed round and round.

"Sometimes things aren't as obvious as they seem. You have to look deeper to find out what the true problem is."

Miss Alaska's words echoed in Primrose's head but what did her teacher mean? Primrose had to work it out to help poor Sammy. If she didn't, Sammy would stay sad and she'd fail her first task. It was a shocking thought to clever Primrose.

"Maybe I'm not so clever," she wondered aloud.

The little Fairy Bear on the roundabout was bouncing up and down.

"Faster," he shouted, waving a paw and accidentally letting go of his wand. The toy wand flew through the air, bounced on the ground and slid under the roundabout. The Fairy Bear slowed the roundabout with his paw then jumped off. He lay on his tummy and tried to reach the wand, but his arms weren't long enough and he burst into tears.

On the stone bench his mother jumped up in alarm.

"Rufus!" she cried, rushing over. "What happened?"

The mother gathered the howling Fairy Bear into her arms, patting his back as she searched for an injury. Primrose jumped off her swing and rushed over.

Chapter Five

Primrose tried to get the mother's attention to tell her what had happened. "He's not hurt – he's lost his wand."

But she didn't seem to hear her, so Primrose pointed her wand at the bottom of the roundabout and chanted.

"Toy wand, come to me,
At the count of one, two, THREE!"

Warmth rushed through the silver stem of Primrose's wand. The triangular jade jewel

sparkled then three green stars whizzed out
and disappeared under the roundabout.
There was a funny squeaking noise and
suddenly the toy wand slid out from where
it'd been lost and came to rest at Primrose's
paws. She picked it up and handed it to
Rufus, who immediately stopped crying.

"Oh, Rufus! You gave me such a fright.
I thought you'd hurt yourself," said the
mother Fairy Bear with relief.

"Thank you," said Rufus, beaming at
Primrose.

"Yes, thank you," his mum added.

"You're welcome," said Primrose,
glad that she'd made someone happy.
Thoughtfully she walked back to the
swings. That mother had wrongly thought
Rufus had injured himself playing, whereas
Primrose had been able to help because
she'd seen what had happened. Suddenly
Miss Alaska's words began to make sense.
Primrose had to find out more about
Sammy to discover what was making him
unhappy. Primrose was sure the magic
mirror was giving her a clue by showing
her Lucy at the same time as Sammy. But
how were they linked? Primrose couldn't
work it out. Feeling frustrated she hurried
home. If only it was morning already so
that she could restart her task and find a
way to help Sammy!

★

A Puzzle for Primrose

Primrose woke early and ate a hurried breakfast of honey-soaked toast and nectar juice. She hugged her parents, waved at her brothers (who were too sticky to hug) and set out for the Grand Door. There was hardly anyone else about as it was too early for most Fairy Bears to start work. Primrose flew along the Main Tunnel to the huge Grand Door, which was still closed. On nimble paws she hopped up the gnarled root staircase and reached up for the sycamore-leaf-shaped handle. It was exciting opening the door by herself.

Primrose traced her paw over the wooden handle, feeling the engravings that made it look like a real leaf. Her fur was tingling with anticipation as she pulled open the door, sighing happily as the darkness rushed out to meet her. Bouncing lightly on her paws Primrose leaped into the air and flew up the dark tree trunk until a small circle of light shining through the squirrel hole beckoned her closer. Without stopping Primrose darted through the squirrel hole and turned a joyful somersault as she arrived outside.

It was a glorious morning. The sun spread out across a pale blue sky, spilling light on the colourful flowers scattered across Firefly Meadow. Primrose took a deep breath, inhaling the fresh morning air and the perfume of the flowers. She was determined to take things more slowly today, and find out exactly what was wrong with Sammy. At last she set off on her journey, her green wings beating so

fast she could have been mistaken for a
dragonfly zipping through the air.

It was still early morning when she flew
over Sammy's bungalow. Dipping down
Primrose was just in time to see the front
door open a crack.

"Out you go," said an elderly voice.

Sammy's whiskery face squeezed through
the door, his nose twitching as he sampled
the morning air.

"Hurry up!" said Mrs Parker, with a note
of impatience this time.

Casually Sammy walked into the front
garden
and
began
to sniff
under
the
bushes.

For a moment Primrose was cross. Lazy Mrs Parker! Why didn't she take Sammy for a walk instead of just putting him out in the garden? Dogs loved going on walks and there was a park nearby. Primrose had just flown over it. Suddenly, remembering Rufus and the lost wand, Primrose checked her thoughts. She mustn't jump to conclusions. There might be a good reason for Mrs Parker's behaviour and it was up to Primrose to find out the facts. She would go and see Lucy first. Maybe she could help.

Leaving Sammy snuffling in the bushes, Primrose soared quickly across the road to Lucy's house. The front door was closed so Primrose flew around the house, peering in the windows. There was no sign of Lucy downstairs, only her mum, typing away at a computer in a room with a huge desk and lots of bookcases. Starting at the front

of the house Primrose flew up to the first-
floor windows. She found Lucy straight
away, lying on her tummy in the middle of
her bedroom, reading a book about dogs.
The window was open so Primrose went
inside and landed on a picture of a dog that
looked like Sammy.

"Primrose!" Lucy was surprised and delighted to see her. "Have you come to play with me?"

"Not today," said Primrose honestly. "I've come back because I haven't finished my task and I hoped you might be able to help me."

"Me?" Lucy's brown eyes shone. "I'd love to. What do you want me to do?"

Primrose explained about Sammy and how she thought she'd solved the problem of his unhappiness but hadn't. When she'd finished, Lucy got up and stood beside the window looking out on to the street.

"I used to see Mrs Parker out with Sammy every day," she said thoughtfully. "But lately she hardly goes out at all. She wasn't very friendly when I took Sammy back yesterday. Usually she talks for ages. She loves hearing about school and all the things I've been doing, but yesterday she was acting strangely. She opened the door just enough to see who it was then made poor Sammy squeeze inside. Maybe she doesn't want him any more. It's not fair! I'd love to have a dog."

Surely Mrs Parker hadn't grown tired of Sammy? Primrose didn't want to believe that. There had to be another reason. She fluttered over to the window and landed on Lucy's hand.

"Look," said Lucy suddenly. "What's Sammy doing? He's got his head under the fence."

"He must have dug a hole," said Primrose. "Quick, Lucy! He's escaping again."

Primrose darted through the open window and into the street while Lucy ran downstairs. Sammy's head and shoulders were already through the hole and he wriggled like a stuck snake as he tried to get the rest of his body through. Across the street Lucy's front door opened and she heard Lucy call out to her mum, "Sammy's escaped again. Can I go after him?"

Primrose didn't hear the reply because at that moment Sammy gave a satisfied grunt and, wriggling free, he set off down the road. His tail was just disappearing round the corner as Lucy came outside and carefully crossed over to Mrs Parker's house.

"He went that way," said Primrose, pointing.

"Let's go," said Lucy, setting off at a fast jog.

58

A Puzzle for Primrose

She ran down the road, while Primrose flew alongside her. Reaching the corner they saw Sammy at the end of the next road.

"Sammy!" called Lucy, but the little dog kept going, his tail wagging cheerfully as he galumphed along.

"He's heading towards the park where Mrs Parker used to walk him," panted Lucy at the end of the next street. She ran

fast and Primrose frantically beat her wings to keep up. Soon they reached the park and Lucy stepped through the iron gates shouting, "Sammy, here, boy!"

The park was full of children playing, and dogs on leads sedately walking alongside their owners, but there was no sign of Sammy anywhere.

Chapter Six

Primrose wasn't happy about flying low over such a crowded place.

"Can I ride on your shoulder so your hair hides me?" she asked Lucy.

"I'd love that!" Lucy replied excitedly.

Primrose flew down and hid behind Lucy's long black hair, using her wand to part the hair enough for her to peek out. Lucy jogged round the park calling Sammy's name. About halfway round she stopped suddenly and reached down, pulling a tartan collar with a round metal disc attached out of a flower bed.

"Oh no!" she gasped. "It's Sammy's collar. It must have fallen off. We've got to find him quickly. Mrs Parker's address is on this tag. If Sammy gets lost, then no one will know where he lives so they won't be able to take him home."

"It looks like he went that way," Primrose said, pointing at the trampled flowers.

"Yes, it does," Lucy agreed.

She picked her way through the flower bed, being careful not to cause any more damage as she followed Sammy's paw prints.

"Look!" Lucy gasped at the overturned litter bin lying across the path. "I bet Sammy did that too."

She went to pick it up but Primrose stopped her.

"Let me," she said.

Checking there was no one around Primrose pointed her wand at the bin and chanted.

> *"Stand up, bin,*
> *Litter back in."*

Warmth flooded through her wand as a river of stars burst from the end. The

bin began to rock, faster and faster until
suddenly it tipped itself the right way up
and set itself back on
the path. The
scattered rubbish
magically
came to life
and danced
up in the
air, before
jumping inside
the bin.

   "Cool!"
breathed Lucy. "If only we could use your
magic to find Sammy."

   "Sorry, but it's not strong enough to do
that," said Primrose, her wings drooping.

   "Don't be sorry. There are lots of things
I haven't learned to do yet. Your magic is
brilliant," said Lucy kindly.

"Do you think so?"

"Yes," said Lucy firmly.

They searched the rest of the park, hurriedly putting to right any damage Sammy had caused. There was a knocked over bicycle, two more overturned dustbins and lots of trampled flowers.

"He's not here," sighed Lucy, her eyes bright with unshed tears.

"He can't have gone far," said Primrose, sounding more positive than she felt. "Let's look one more time."

Suddenly Primrose's ears began to twitch. What was that sound? She listened carefully until she heard it again.

"Woof, woof, woof."

"Sammy," shouted Lucy and Primrose together.

"It's coming from the duck pond," said Primrose.

Lucy wheeled round and gasped as she noticed the duck house on the island in the middle of the pond.

"Oh, Sammy, now what have you done?"

"He's stuck!" Primrose started to giggle and so did Lucy and soon neither of them could stop. Naughty Sammy had the ducks' metal water bowl wedged on his head, making him too big to get out of the duck house.

"Now what?" said Lucy, hiccupping with laughter. "Do you think the water's shallow enough for me to wade over and rescue him?"

"You'd better ask a grown-up to help you," said Primrose sensibly. "What about that man over there wearing a uniform?"

"That's the park warden," said Lucy. "Hide under my hair, Primrose, and I'll go and ask him for help."

Luckily the park warden was very nice and didn't get cross when Lucy explained how Sammy was stuck in the duck house. He fetched a pair of waders from his hut and put them on, ready to rescue Sammy.

"Eeek," laughed the warden, handing the soggy dog over to Lucy. "I'm wetter from being licked than I am from being in the pond."

"Thank you," said Lucy gratefully. With nimble fingers she fastened Sammy's collar back round his neck. The park warden lent her a dog lead he kept in his hut, especially for lost dogs, and Lucy thanked him again.

"Take care walking him home," joked the warden. "He's a tiny terror that one. He's probably bored. You ought to take him out more."

"Sammy's not mine. But I'll tell his

owner. And thanks for the loan of the dog lead," she added.

Once they had left the park Primrose came out of hiding and flew alongside Lucy. Sammy seemed very happy, bouncing along at the end of the lead, and Lucy was ecstatic.

"This is the first time I've ever walked a dog," she smiled. "If I had my own dog, I'd take him for walks every day, even in the rain!"

They turned the corner into the end of Lucy's road and Primrose noticed that both Lucy and Sammy seemed to slow down as if neither of them wanted the walk to be over. By the time they reached Mrs Parker's gate they were crawling along like two snails. Primrose fluttered down and hid on Lucy's shoulder again when she knocked on Mrs Parker's door. Mrs Parker took ages to answer. Primrose was glad. It gave her extra time to think about her task. She'd rescued Sammy twice now, but she still hadn't found out why the little dog was unhappy. Primrose gave a big sigh. All her friends had completed their tasks in two days. This was Primrose's second day and

she was still no closer to solving the puzzle. Would Miss Alaska give her extra time? It would be embarrassing to take longer than everyone else to complete her first task, but it would be much better than failing it. Failing would mean spending an extra year in the juniors. Primrose's green wings went ice cold at the thought.

Chapter Seven

Once again Mrs Parker didn't open the front door fully and made poor Sammy squeeze inside.

"Thank you," she said shortly, then closed the door with a bang.

"Well!" Lucy was outraged. "What's wrong with her? She used to be so nice."

Primrose came out of hiding and hovered near Lucy's face.

"Mrs Parker's got a secret. Did you notice the way her eyes kept wandering to something hidden behind the door?"

A Puzzle for Primrose

"Oh! I just thought she wasn't being very friendly," said Lucy. "I wonder what she's got to hide."

"I'll take a look," Primrose offered.

Primrose flew round the bungalow peeping in all the windows until she'd circled the whole house. Lucy was sitting on the doorstep waiting for her to return.

"Well?" she asked, jumping up.

Primrose shook her head. "All the curtains were drawn so I couldn't see a thing. But there is another way."

Primrose pointed her wand at the letter box.

Fairy Bears

"Letter box, letter box, open wide,
And let this Fairy Bear fly inside."

In a flash of green a flurry of stars cascaded
from Primrose's wand and landed on the
letter box. Primrose held her breath. Had
the spell been strong enough to work? Very
slowly the letter box began to open until
it was wide enough for Primrose to fly
through. Then the flap stopped moving and
held itself out, so it looked like a tongue
poking from the letter box's
metal mouth.

A Puzzle for Primrose

"Wow! Primrose you're so clever," whispered Lucy.

Primrose blushed. Being clever didn't feel as important as it used to. It was how you used your knowledge that counted.

"I won't be long," she whispered back, taking a deep breath and trying to steady her nerves as she flew inside Mrs Parker's house.

The drawn curtains made it very dark inside but Primrose liked that. Mrs Parker's house felt small and cluttered compared to Lucy's. Every surface was covered with photographs of Sammy and ornaments of dogs. Mrs Parker was obviously keen on dogs so what was going on? There were only four rooms and a tiny bathroom so it didn't take long for Primrose to explore. Knowing Mrs Parker was in the kitchen Primrose investigated that room last. Her heart thumped nervously and her wings trembled as she flew inside, keeping close to the ceiling where she wouldn't be spotted.

Mrs Parker was leaning on the kitchen worktop, waiting for a kettle to boil. Her gnarled hands gripped the counter tightly and her face was creased with pain. Leaning against her was a walking stick. Sammy lay on a tartan blanket, eyes closed and grunting contentedly after his adventure in the park.

Primrose flew nearer. There was a crude bandage round Mrs Parker's leg that didn't look like it had been put on by a doctor or nurse. The kettle boiled and switched itself off with a loud click that made Primrose jump.

It took Mrs Parker ages to make herself a drink. She had to put the kettle down three times to steady herself. Using the stick for support she shuffled out of the kitchen, the drink wobbling in the cup as she slowly made her way to her lounge.

Primrose had seen enough. Quickly she flew back through the letter box, which closed behind her. Lucy was still waiting on the step.

"You were a long time," she said anxiously.

"Mrs Parker's hurt her leg," said Primrose. "She's using a stick and she can hardly walk."

"So that's why she hasn't been taking Sammy out!" Lucy exclaimed.

"Hmm," mused Primrose as an idea began to shape in her mind. "Lucy, why don't you offer to walk Sammy for Mrs Parker? Then

she wouldn't have to leave him out in the garden where he gets bored and lonely."

"That's a brilliant idea. I'd have to ask Mum first, but I'm sure she'd say yes. It'll be like having my own dog!" said Lucy happily. "I'll go and ask her right now!"

Lucy's mum thought it was a great idea too.

"Tell Mrs Parker that if she needs anything from the shops I'll get it for her. I'll also drive her to the doctor's if she wants to see one," she added.

"Thanks, Mum."

Lucy's eyes sparkled merrily as she went back to their neighbour's house with Primrose flying beside her. Primrose hid in a bush when Lucy knocked on the door. She waited impatiently even though she knew it would take Mrs Parker ages to answer with her hurt leg. At last there came the sound of shuffling and the front door opened a crack.

"Hello, Lucy, what is it this time?" said Mrs Parker irritably.

Lucy flushed and suddenly became tongue tied. Primrose hoped she'd remember that Mrs Parker was grumpy because she was in pain.

"I was wondering if you'd like any help walking and grooming Sammy?" said Lucy in a rush. "It's the half-term holiday so I've got lots of free time."

Mrs Parker stared at Lucy for a moment then her wrinkled face broke into a huge smile.

"That would be marvellous," she said. "I've hurt my leg, you see, and I can't get out. Poor Sammy's rather sad. He does love his walks."

"Mum says she'll get your shopping and take you to the doctor's."

Primrose groaned. How was Lucy going
to explain that she knew about Mrs Parker's
leg? But she needn't have worried. Mrs
Parker burst out laughing until she had to
reach for her walking stick hidden behind
the door to steady herself.

A Puzzle for Primrose

"I thought I'd managed to keep that a secret," she chortled. "I was worried that if anyone found out I couldn't take Sammy for walks they'd think it was cruel and take him away from me. I didn't want that to happen. Sammy's all I've got."

"Poor you," said Lucy sympathetically. "But you can always ask me when you need help. I love dogs, especially cute ones like Sammy."

"Thank you, Lucy. You can borrow Sammy any time you like. He's always happy to go on a walk."

Lucy arranged to take Sammy for another walk to the park that afternoon so she could return the borrowed dog lead. Mrs Parker looked much happier as she said goodbye.

"It's time for me to go," said Primrose, once they were back in Lucy's garden.

"I'm going to really miss you," sighed Lucy. "But at least I've got Sammy to keep me company. I can't wait to walk him this afternoon. I'm going to ask Mrs Parker if I can borrow his brush and groom him afterwards."

"He'll love that," said Primrose. Then she added, "I'm going to miss you too. Thank you for helping me with my task."

Primrose's stomach fizzed with excitement. She'd done it. She'd finally discovered what Sammy's problem was and by fixing it she'd completed her first task. With Lucy's help, of course! The task had made Primrose realize that everyone needs help sometimes. Fluttering into the air Primrose hovered in front of Lucy's face.

"There's one last thing before I go." With a grand sweep of her wand

A Puzzle for Primrose

Primrose recited a friendship spell she'd learned back in Cub Class.

"From me to you,
A star that's true!"

Primrose's wand began to tremble until suddenly with a loud crack a bright green star popped out of the end. Catching it in both paws she offered it to Lucy.

"A friendship star," she said simply.

"Thank you!" Lucy's eyes were as round as dinner plates as she carefully took the star from Primrose.

"I'll keep it in my jewellery box and look at it every day."

"Bye, Lucy." Primrose fluttered higher.

"Bye!" Lucy waved back, smiling.

Primrose could feel Lucy's eyes watching her as she rose into the air. She wasn't usually impulsive and she didn't want to show off but she couldn't help herself. With

an extra beat of her wings she turned three somersaults and two cartwheels. Hearing Lucy chuckle Primrose giggled too.

Primrose couldn't wait to tell Miss Alaska how by learning not to jump to conclusions she'd completed her task. Dipping her wings in a final goodbye, Primrose flew home to the Crystal Caves.

Primrose

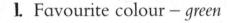

1. Favourite colour – *green*

    2. Favourite gemstone – *peridot*

3. Best flower – *primrose*

    4. Cutest animal – *rabbit*

5. Birthday month – *April*

    6. Yummiest food – *honeycomb*

7. Favourite place – *School Caves*

    8. Hobbies – *solving puzzles*

9. Best ever season – *spring*

    10. Worst thing – *laziness*